Copyright © 2002 by Nord-Süd Verlag AG, Gossau Zürich, Switzerland
First published in Switzerland under the title *Marike wird die Geister los*.
English translation copyright © 2002 by North-South Books Inc., New York

First published in the United States, Great Britain, Canada,
Australia, and New Zealand in 2002 by North-South Books,
an imprint of Nord-Süd Verlag AG, Gossau Zürich, Switzerland.

Distributed in the United States by North-South Books Inc., New York.

Library of Congress Cataloging-in-Publication Data is available.
A CIP catalogue record for this book is available from The British Library.
ISBN 0-7358-1704-9 (trade edition)   10 9 8 7 6 5 4 3 2 1
ISBN 0-7358-1705-7 (library edition)   10 9 8 7 6 5 4 3 2 1
Printed in Belgium

For more information about our books, and the authors and artists
who create them, visit our web site: www.northsouth.com

Miranda's Ghosts

By Udo Weigelt · Illustrated by Christa Unzner

Translated by Marisa Miller

NORTH-SOUTH BOOKS · NEW YORK / LONDON

Miranda was on her way home from
the Halloween party, marching along
happily, still wearing the terrific
witch's mask she'd made, when
suddenly she remembered the ghosts.
  She knew they'd be back again
tonight, stirring up all kinds of trouble.

Once again, she'd
be so frightened, she'd
have to hide under the
covers, shivering with
fear while the ghosts
danced wildly around
her room.

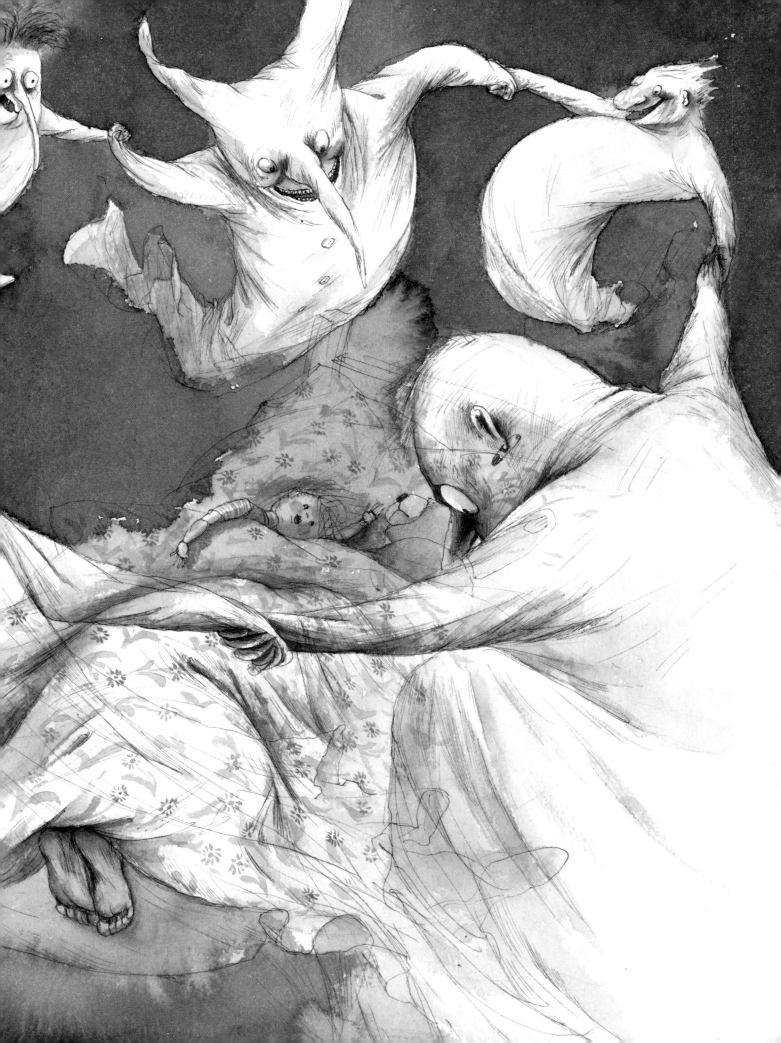

That night just before bedtime, Miranda picked up her witch's mask and studied it for a while. It certainly was scary. Then Miranda made a decision. "I've had enough!" she declared. "I'm going to get rid of those ghosts once and for all!" She put on the mask and hid behind the armchair in her bedroom.

Before long, the ghosts appeared. One crawled out from under the bed, another came out of the closet, a third crept out from behind the curtain. A new one that she'd never seen before climbed out of the toy chest.

When they started dancing around the room, Miranda jumped out from behind the couch. She was very scared, but she was also very determined.

When the ghosts saw her witch's mask and heard Miranda's eerie howl, they shrank back and huddled together in fear. They all turned as white as sheets.

"I've had it with you!" Miranda said sternly. "I'm tired of being scared. Just leave me alone!"

And with that, the ghosts grew a little bit smaller.

Miranda took off her mask.

"Hey, you, Ghost-from-under-the-Bed! Get over here!" she commanded. "How dare you try to scare me!" Miranda gave the Ghost-from-under-the-Bed a nice long talking-to.

The ghost dropped his head in shame. He shrank even more. The others did, too.

"You rude creatures need to
be tamed like circus animals!"
said Miranda.

The ghosts were stunned. No
one had ever dared to speak to
them like that before.

The ghosts were so intimidated, they did whatever Miranda ordered them to do—they gave her piggyback rides, rolled over and begged, jumped through hoops, and played haunted circus with her.

And as they played, the ghosts became smaller
and smaller until finally they were as small and light
as feathers and Miranda could fit them all in one hand.

Miranda opened the window, took a deep breath,
and blew those ghosts right out into the dark night.

They swirled and twirled down to the ground,
turning into crumpled white leaves that landed softly
in a little pile.

The next morning Miranda hung her witch's mask over her bed. Then she went outside, raked the tiny white leaves together, and tossed them away. "That's the end of that!" she declared happily.

And it was indeed, the end of Miranda's ghosts.

E
WEIGELT

Weigelt, Udo.
Miranda's ghosts.

$15.95

DATE			